美玲打嗝

Mei Ling's Hiccups

By David Mills
Illustrated by Derek Brazell

Mandarin translation by Frank Wang

MANTRA
LINGUA

"谁想去做派对游戏？"美玲的老师问道。

"Who wants to play party games?" asked Mei Ling's teacher.

"跟我来！"他唱起歌来。

"Follow me!" he sang.

可是，美玲想喝完她的果汁。
这果汁又凉，
又好喝，
她喝得一滴都不剩。

But Mei Ling wanted to finish her drink.
It was cool.
It was yummy.
And she drank every last drop!

可是刚一喝完果汁，
她就打起嗝来："呃！"

But when she'd finished
All she could say was ... "Hicc!"

接下来又是一声"呃！"
紧接着又是"呃！"

And another one came: "Hicc!"
And another: "Hicc!"

噢，糟了！

Oh no!

班咯咯地笑起来。
美玲也想大声笑，
可是她只能……"呃！"

Ben giggled.
Mei Ling wanted to laugh too
But all she could say was... "Hicc!"

"我知道，我知道！"班说，
"我妈妈说你要这样做……
从一数到五。"

"I know. I know!" said Ben.
"My mum says you have to do this...
and count to five."

So they both plugged their noses.
1   2   3   4   5 and ...
"HICC! Oh no!" said Mei Ling

于是他俩都捏住了鼻子，
"一，二，三，四，五……
"呃！噢，不行！"美玲说。

这时茹贝走进来。
"我知道，我知道！"茹贝说，
"我爸爸说你要这样做……"

Then Ruby came back in.
"I know. I know!" said Ruby.
"My dad says you have to do this ..."

于是大家都努力地低下头倒着看
一，二，三，四，五……
"呃… 噢，不行！"美玲说。

So everyone tried to look upside down.
1 2 3 4 5 and ...
"HICC! Oh no!" said Mei Ling.

这时利奥走进来。
"我知道，我知道！"利奥说，
"我叔叔说你要这样做……"

Then Leo came back in.
"I know I know!" said Leo.
"My uncle says you have to do this ..."

于是大家都从被子的另一边喝水。
一，二，三，四，五……
"呃……噢，不行！"美玲说。

So everyone drank water from the other
side of their cups.
1   2   3   4   5 and ...
"HICC... Oh no!" said Mei Ling.

这时萨希走进来。
"我知道，我知道！"萨希说，
"我奶奶说你要这样做……"

Then Sahil came back in.
"I know I know!" said Sahil.
"My grandma says you have to do this ..."

于是大家都转呀转呀打转转。
一，二，三，四，五……
"呃……噢，不行！"美玲说。

So everyone went spin spin spin.
1 2 3 4 5 and ...
"HICC ... Oh no!" said Mei Ling.

这时苏菲走进来。
"我知道，我知道！"
"我表姐说你要这样做……"

Then Sophie came back in.
"I know I know!" said Sophie.
"My cousin says you have to do this ..."

于是大家都做骑自行车的动作。
一，二，三，四，五……
"呃……噢，不行！"美玲说。

So everyone did bicycles in the air.
1   2   3   4   5   and ...
"HICC ... Oh no!" said Mei Ling.

这时她看到她的气球，
于是有了个主意。
"我知道了，"她慢慢地说。
"美玲！"她的朋友们都喊起来。

But then she saw her balloon and she had an idea.
"I know," she said slowly.
"Mei Ling!" shouted all her friends.

啪！
美玲的气球爆了。

POP!
went Mei Ling's balloon.

"嘘！" 大家都静下来听美玲是不是还打嗝。

"Shhhhh!" Everyone listened carefully for Mei Ling's hiccups.

” 不打嗝了？ ” 美玲轻声地问。

"Gone?" asked Mei Ling very quietly.

"不打嗝了！ ” 大家说。

"Gone!" said everyone.

"太棒了！"大家都欢呼起来。

"HURRAY!" shouted everyone.

啪！ 啪！ 啪！ 啪！ 这时候……

POP!　　POP!　　POP!　　POP!　　POP!　　And ...

"这是怎么回事？"老师问。

"What was that?" asked the teacher.

"呃！"大家都打了个嗝。
"噢，糟了！"美玲说。

"HICC!" said everyone.
"OH NO!" said Mei Ling.

For the children of Harry Roberts Nursery,

D.M.

For all the great children and staff of Soho Parish School,
and for Hilary, my lovely supportive mum, with love,

D.B.

First published 2000 by Mantra Lingua Ltd
Global House, 303 Ballards Lane,
London, N12 8NP, UK
http://www.mantralingua.com

This edition published 2014

Text copyright © 2000 David Mills
Illustration copyright © 2000 Derek Brazell
Dual language text copyright © 2000 Mantra Lingua Ltd
Audio copyright © 2013 Mantra Lingua Ltd

A CIP record of this book is available from the British Library

Printed in Letchworth,UK FP110414PB04142007